Things We Do

A KIDS' GUIDE TO COMMUNITY ACTIVITY

by Rachelle Kreisman

with illustrations by Tim Haggerty

RED
CHAIR
· PRESS ·

Publisher's Cataloging-In-Publication Data
(Prepared by The Donohue Group, Inc.)

Kreisman, Rachelle.
    Things we do : a kids' guide to community activity / by Rachelle Kreisman ; with illustrations by Tim Haggerty. -- [First edition].

    pages : illustrations ; cm. -- (Start smart: community)

    Summary: In communities we not only find goods and services, but we also find places for fun and enjoyment to keep us happy and healthy. Includes fun facts.
    Interest age level: 006-009.
    Edition statement supplied by publisher.
    Includes index.
    Issued also as an ebook.
    ISBN: 978-1-939656-93-3 (library hardcover)
    ISBN: 978-1-939656-94-0 (paperback)

    1. Community life--Juvenile literature. 2. Parks--Juvenile literature. 3. Theaters--Juvenile literature. 4. Sports--Juvenile literature. 5. Museums--Juvenile literature. 6. Community life. 7. Parks. 8. Theaters. 9. Sports. 10. Museums. I. Haggerty, Tim. II. Title.

HM761 .K743 2015
307   2014957501

Illustration credits: p. 1, 5, 7, 13, 14, 15, 17, 19, 21, 22, 27, 28, 32: Tim Haggerty

Photo credits: Cover, p. 4, 10 (small), 14, 16, 18 (small), 25 (large), 26: iStock; p. 1, 5, 6, 7, 8, 9, 10, 11, 15, 19, 24, 25 (top), 26 (small), 27, 31: Shutterstock; p. 12, 13: Berkshire Theater Group; p. 17, 18 (large), 20, 22, 23, 29, 32: Dreamstime; p. 21: Bob Gambling Photo, Courtesy of the SoNo Switch Tower Museum; p. 32: Courtesy of the author, Rachelle Kreisman

This series first published by:
Red Chair Press LLC   PO Box 333   South Egremont, MA 01258-0333

Printed in the United States of America

042015 1P WRZF15

Table of Contents

Words in **bold type** are defined in the glossary.

CHAPTER 1

Community

Think about your neighborhood. What do you see? You may see people, pets, and homes. You may also see buildings, roads, cars, and trees. Your neighborhood is part of a **community**. A community is a place where people live, work, and play.

Some communities are busy cities. Others have fewer people and more land. What do they all have in common? They have places to meet people's needs. Those places include schools, hospitals, gas stations, and banks.

Do you like to have fun? You are not alone! Many people in a community work hard. They also like to do fun activities. Communities have places where people can go to do just that! Parks, movie theaters, and ice skating rinks are just a few of those places. Keep reading to learn more about the fun you can have in a community.

CHAPTER 2

Parks

Most communities have parks. They are outdoor spaces for the **public** to enjoy. Community parks are usually owned and operated by the city or state. The parks have trees for shade, grass, and flowers. They also have benches so people can sit and relax.

Parks often have playgrounds for kids. Play on the slide, swings, and monkey bars. You can also bring a ball or Frisbee to play catch. Walk, play tag, and run around. Going to the park is good exercise!

What else can you do at a park? Lots of things! Pack a lunch and have a picnic. Many parks have picnic tables. If not, bring a blanket and sit on the grass. Enjoy your food while you breathe the fresh air. Look up at the sky and see what cloud shapes you can find. Talk to others, read a book, or play a game. It's all up to you!

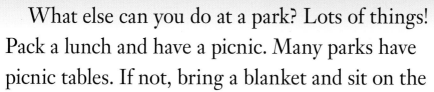

JUST JOKING!

Q: What did the big flower say to the small flower?

A: Hi, little bud!

Every park is different. Some have trails to go biking or hiking. People can explore and study nature. Check out plants, flowers, and insects. Bring binoculars to be a bird-watcher.

Some parks are near the beach. Other parks are in busy cities. Dog parks are made just for people with dogs. Owners may take their dogs to play there with other dogs.

🏠 Exercise is good for *dogs and owners*.

DID YOU KNOW?

You can bike, walk, and run while helping others. How? Take part in a charity race. People who enter pay a fee. They also ask others to donate money. The money goes to help a good cause.

Some communities have **national parks**. A national park is an area of land set aside and owned by a national government. The U.S. National Park Service manages the national parks in the United States. Parks Canada manages important parks in Canada. National parks protect land and wild animals. Those animals include many **endangered species**.

National parks are for everyone to enjoy. They receive millions of visitors each year.

⌂ This tree in Sequoia Giant Forest National Park is the world's largest.

FUN FACT

What is the world's first national park? Yellowstone National Park! The land was set aside to be protected in 1872. With more than 2 million acres, the park is huge. It is larger than the states of Rhode Island and Delaware put together! Most of Yellowstone is located in Wyoming. A small area of the park is in Montana and Idaho.

GENERAL SHERMAN

CHAPTER 3

Movie Theaters

Do you like going to the movies? Lots of people do! Not all movie theaters are the same. A theater can be small and show only a few movies. Theaters can also be huge and show more than 20 movies at a time!

Some communities show movies outdoors. People can bring a blanket or chair and enjoy the movie while sitting on the grass. A few communities even have drive-in theaters. People watch the movie while sitting inside their cars.

DID YOU KNOW?

Drive-in movie theaters were popular in the 1950s and 1960s. At the time, the United States had more than 4,000 drive-ins. Today, fewer than 400 remain.

Another kind of movie theater is the IMAX. It stands for *Image MAXimum*. The images are shown on a giant curved screen. It is much larger than the screen at a regular movie theater. In addition, the IMAX movie images have more details.

Many IMAX theaters show **3-D** movies as well. Special 3-D glasses make you feel like you are part of the movie, not just watching it. Many regular movie theaters also show 3-D movies.

CHAPTER 4

Live Theater

Nothing can take the place of live theater. Theaters are places where people perform shows for an audience. The shows take place on a stage. Shows can be plays, concerts, or dance performances.

Each visit to the theater is special. Plays can be serious or funny. Concerts feature different kinds of music. Dancers perform many styles of dance. A musical is a kind of play that combines all three. It tells a story with music, song, and dance.

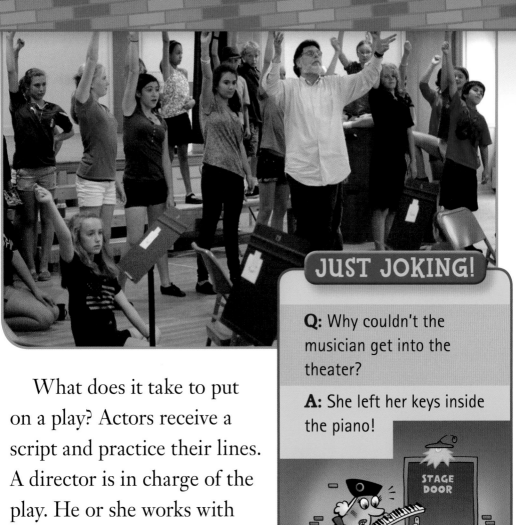

JUST JOKING!

Q: Why couldn't the musician get into the theater?

A: She left her keys inside the piano!

STAGE DOOR

What does it take to put on a play? Actors receive a script and practice their lines. A director is in charge of the play. He or she works with the actors and decides how the play should be presented.

Designers build the scenery and create the costumes. People also make or find **props** for the show. Props are the objects used on stage, such as a telephone or books. The scenery and props used on the stage are called the **set**.

The actors spend weeks or months preparing. The final practices are called **dress rehearsals**. The actors perform in costume, without their scripts. Lighting and sound operators control the stage lights and sound effects.

On opening night, the actors go to their dressing rooms. They put on their costumes and get their makeup done. Audience members arrive and take their seats.

DID YOU KNOW?

The areas to the left and right of the stage are the wings. They are hidden from the audience's view. Actors stand in the wings until it is time to go on stage.

Each audience member receives a **program** at the door. A program is a booklet that tells about the show, the schedule, and the performers.

Now, it is time for the show! The actors do a great job. When it is over, they take a bow. Audience members clap their hands to show they liked the play.

TRY THIS!

Get together with friends to put on a play. Start by choosing your favorite story and write a list of the characters. Then write a script. Decide who will play each character and practice reading your lines. Practice some more! Make costumes and have a dress rehearsal. When you are ready, put on a show for family and friends.

CHAPTER 5

Sports

If you like sports, you are in luck! Communities often have places to play and watch sports. Many have soccer and baseball fields. Kids can join local teams to play. Family and friends can go to the games and cheer them on.

Are you a fan of basketball or tennis? Some communities have courts for those sports. Do you like to swim? A public pool or beach may be nearby. You may also be able to take swim lessons.

Some communities have ice-skating rinks. Kids and adults can ice skate or play ice hockey. You can rent skates or bring your own. Indoor rinks are open all year long. Outdoor rinks are open during cold weather.

Public skate times are set aside for anyone who wants to skate. Music is often played at these sessions. Rinks also offer lessons for all ages. You can learn how to skate or play ice hockey.

JUST JOKING!

Q: What month is the coldest?

A: Decembrrr!

BRRR!

🏠 Hockey is great fun in winter months.

Do you like to skateboard? Some communities have skate parks. Kids can go there to practice their skateboard skills. A skate park is usually made of concrete. It has ramps, stairs, and ledges. Beginner areas have slower slopes and smaller obstacles. Advanced skaters can speed around more difficult courses.

Communities may also have roller rinks. Kids can roller skate or inline skate there. The rinks often play music so you can move to the beat.

Millions of people are sports fans. Along with playing sports, they like to watch the pros play. Some communities have college or professional teams. Athletes play at large stadiums and arenas, which can seat thousands of fans.

People can buy tickets to the games. Fans often wear team colors or **jerseys** to support their teams. Many of the games can also be seen on television so supporters can follow their community teams.

DID YOU KNOW?

The game that Americans call soccer is called football by most other countries.

CHAPTER 6

Museums

Spend time at a museum. It's a great way to learn new things! A museum is a building in which objects of interest are displayed for the public. The objects are often of art, science, or history. A collection of objects is an **exhibit**.

Most large museums are located in big cities. One of the most popular is the National Museum of Natural History. It is a science museum in Washington, D.C.

♠ The Museum of Natural History is featured in the movie *Night at the Museum.*

FUN FACT

The National Museum of Natural History is huge. It is more than 1 million square feet! That's as big as 20 football fields. The museum's collection includes about 125 million objects.

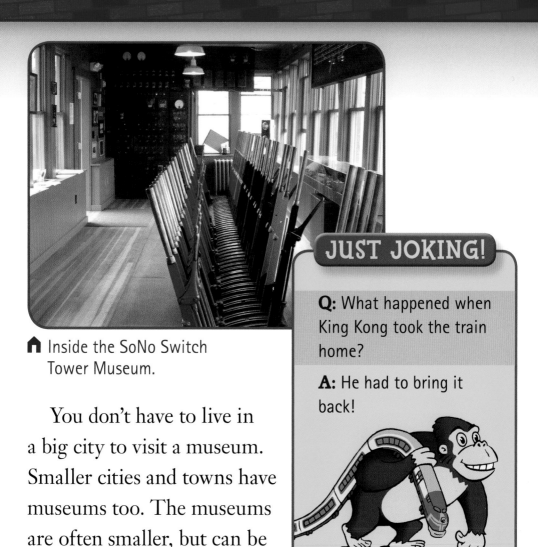

↑ Inside the SoNo Switch Tower Museum.

You don't have to live in a big city to visit a museum. Smaller cities and towns have museums too. The museums are often smaller, but can be just as interesting.

The SoNo Switch Tower Museum in South Norwalk, Connecticut is tiny. It is located in an old railroad switch tower built in 1896. People once worked in the tower to switch trains from one track to another. Visitors climb the many steel stairs to get inside. There, they learn about train history.

Once inside a museum, take a look around. With so much to see, you may not know where to start. No problem! Museums often have maps and tours. A tour guide can lead the way and tell you about the exhibits. He or she can also answer questions.

Some museums also have audio guides. You can listen to recordings as you visit each exhibit.

🏠 Docents are guides who can tell you many interesting facts about exhibits.

NEWSEUM NEWS

🏠 The interactive news media museum, Newseum, opened in Washington D.C. in 2008.

What exhibits will you find inside a museum? It depends on where you go. From art to sports, each museum is different. You may see paintings at one museum. You may learn about dinosaurs or insects at another.

Collections can include so many things: photos, doll houses, rocks, shells, or puppets. The list goes on and on. Some communities even have children's museums. They have hands-on exhibits just for kids. Check out what museums are in or near your community!

CHAPTER 7

Community Centers

A community center is a place where people in a community gather. Centers have activities, programs, and special events. Some have fitness rooms, pools, and sports programs. They usually offer classes for all ages. Classes may include dance, arts and crafts, music, and theater.

Community centers often have programs for kids. Many centers host summer camps too.

🏠 Community centers can be a safe place to try new activities.

Some community centers are for certain age groups. Youth centers are places for kids to have fun and make new friends. Senior centers are just for **senior citizens**. Seniors often have to be age 60 and older to join. Some senior centers like to have kids visit and make friends.

Religious groups may have community centers too. The centers have activities similar to other community centers. Plus, they celebrate holidays of that religion. They also offer classes about the religion and culture.

DID YOU KNOW?

Like other community centers, senior centers often have fitness programs and classes for arts and crafts.

CHAPTER 8

So Much to Do

Communities have so many things to do. It makes life much more fun and interesting. If you feel bored, turn to your community. Take a walk in a park. Play on the playground. Visit a museum and learn something new. Go to a theater and see a play or a movie. Join a sports team or watch a game. Sign up for a class at a community center. You might even visit a senior center.

What are you waiting for? Take part in all your community has to offer! Not only will you have fun, you may also make new friends. Then you can all have fun in the community together. What do you get when you add fun and friends? A happy, healthy life!

TRY THIS!

Each community has places to have fun. How many other things can you do in your community for fun? (Here is a hint to get started: Where can you go bowling?)

Glossary

community: a place where people live, work, and play

docent: a museum tour guide

dress rehearsal: the final practice of a play in full costume and makeup

endangered species: animals or plants in danger of dying out

exhibit: a collection of objects in a museum

jersey: a shirt worn as part of a sports uniform

national park: an area of land set aside and owned by a national government

program: a booklet that tells about a show, schedule, and performers

props: the objects used on stage, such as a telephone or books

public: all the people making up a community, state, or country

senior citizen: an older person, often 60 and older

set: the scenery and props used on stage during a play

3-D: something that has three-dimensions (height, width, and depth)

What Did You Learn?

See how much you learned about things to do in a community. Answer *true* or *false* for each statement below. Write your answers on a separate piece of paper.

1 Communities have places to meet people's needs.
True or false?

2 A roller rink is a place where kids can ice skate.
True or false?

3 National parks receive millions of visitors each year.
True or false?

4 Most large museums are located in small towns.
True or false?

5 An IMAX theater is a special kind of live theater.
True or false?

For More Information

Books

Caseley, Judith. *On the Town: A Community Adventure.* Greenwillow Books, 2002.

Hayes, Ann. *Meet the Orchestra.* Houghton Mifflin Harcourt, 1995.

Hayes, Ann. *Onstage and Backstage.* Harcourt Brace and Company, 1997.

Kaufman, Gabriel. *Sporting Events: From Baseball to Skateboarding.* Bearport Publishing Company, 2006.

Kalman, Bobbie. *What is a Community from A to Z?* Crabtree Publishing Company, 2000.

Verde, Susan. *The Museum.* Abrams Books for Young Readers, 2013.

Web Sites

CDC: BAM! Body and Mind
http://www.cdc.gov/bam/activity/cards.html

Knowitall.org
http://www.knowitall.org/kidswork/theater/history

National Parks Foundation
http://www.nationalparks.org/connect/npf-kids

National Gallery of Art
http://www.nga.gov/content/ngaweb/education/kids.html

Parks Canada for Kids
http://www.pc.gc.ca/eng/voyage-travel/xplorateurs-xplorers.aspx

Smithsonian Kids
http://www.si.edu/Kids

Note to educators and parents: Our editors have carefully reviewed these web sites to ensure they are suitable for children. Web sites change frequently, however, and we cannot guarantee that a site's future contents will continue to meet our high standards of quality and educational value. You may wish to preview these sites and closely supervise children whenever they access the Internet.

Index

About the Author

Rachelle Kreisman has been a children's writer and editor for many years. She is the author of several children's books and hundreds of *Weekly Reader* classroom magazines. When Rachelle is not writing, she enjoys going to places in her community. She likes taking walks, hiking, biking, kayaking, and doing yoga.

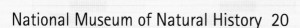

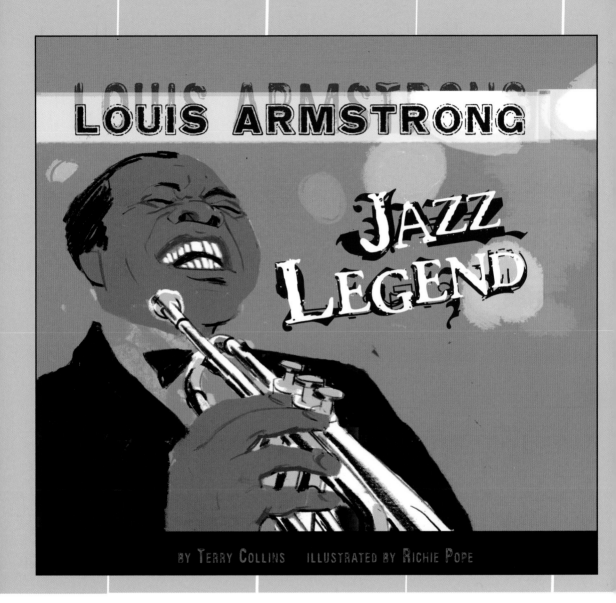

LOUIS ARMSTRONG

JAZZ LEGEND

BY TERRY COLLINS   ILLUSTRATED BY RICHIE POPE

Consultant:
Ricky Riccardi, Archivist
Louis Armstrong House Museum
Queens College, New York

CAPSTONE PRESS
a capstone imprint

Graphic Library is published by Capstone Press.
1710 Roe Crest Drive
North Mankato, Minnesota 56003
www.capstonepub.com

Library of Congress Cataloging-in-Publication Data
Collins, Terry
  Louis Armstrong : jazz legend / by Terry Collins.
     p. cm. – (Graphic library. American graphic)
  Includes bibliographical references and index.
  Summary: "Describes the life of Louis Armstrong, focusing on his rise as a
pop-culture icon"–Provided by publisher.
  ISBN 978-1-4296-8622-8 (library binding)
  ISBN 978-1-4296-9336-3 (paperback)
  ISBN 978-1-62065-267-1 (ebook PDF)
  1. Armstrong, Louis, 1901-1971–Juvenile literature. 2. Jazz musicians–United States–
Biography–Juvenile literature. I. Title.

  ML3930.A75C69 2013
  781.65092–dc23   2011049811

Art Director: Nathan Gassman

Editor: Mari Bolte

Production Specialist: Laura Manthe

Direct quotes appear on the following pages in green:
4, 5, 6, 7, 8, 9, 11, 17, from *Satchmo: My Life in New Orleans* by Louis Armstrong (New York:
   Da Capo Press, Inc., 1986).
10, 12, from *Louis Armstrong: Ambassador Satchmo* by Jean Gay Cornell (Champaign, Ill.:
   Garrard Publishing Company, 1972).
14, 16, 26, 27, from *Louis Armstrong, In His Own Words* by Louis Armstrong. Edited and With
   an Introduction by Thomas Brothers (New York: Oxford University Press, 1999).
22, 23, 25, from *Louis Armstrong: An Extravagent Life* by Laurence Bergreen (New York:
Broadway Books, 1997).

Photo Credit:
Library of Congress: Prints and Photographs Division, 28

Printed in the United States of America in Stevens Point, Wisconsin.
032012   006678WZF12

TABLE of CONTENTS

I was taken to the juvenile court, and then locked up.

CLINK

Louis Armstrong?

Yes, sir.

You're being sent to the Colored Waifs' Home for Boys.

During the New Year's Eve celebration, I had fired my stepfather's pistol over and over into the air.

Making noise for the New Year was an old custom in New Orleans. But not, it seemed, for a 12-year-old colored boy on a public street.

The Waifs' Home was in the country, near a big dairy farm. I, being a city boy, had never seen anything like it.

Captain Jones, who ran things, was a strict man. He drilled us military-style every morning.

SOUND OFF! 1-2!

SOUND OFF! 3-4!

Mr. Alexander taught the boys how to do carpentry, how to garden, and how to build campfires.

Never saw on the line. Cut next to the line to leave material for trimming and finishing.

Mr. Peter Davis taught music.

At first I did not get on very well with Mr. Davis because he did not like the neighborhood I came from.

The little brass band was very good, and Mr. Davis made the boys play a little of every kind of music.

Six months passed, and then, one day he asked ...

Louis Armstrong, how would you like to join our brass band?

I would sit in a corner and listen, enjoying myself immensely.

Mr. Davis started me out on the tambourine ...

... then the bugle ...

... and finally, a few weeks later, the cornet.

I also learned to play the drums.

I got so good at playing the cornet that one day ...

You're going to be the leader of the band, Louis.

The band often got a chance to play at a private picnic or join one of the frequent parades through the streets of New Orleans.

I don't know what would have happened to me without the help of those kind people.

... Ninety-five ... and a nickel makes one dollar.

But Papa Karnofsky, that's too much money.

Use what's left to buy yourself a horn.

How are you going to practice your music if you don't have an instrument?

I wanted to start performing. My friend Buddy Martin said he might have something for me.

My boss is looking for a cornet player. Isn't that what you play?

Yes ... but I don't know if I am good enough to play in a regular band.

Buddy got the gig for me, but now I needed a horn.

Most of the money I earned went to help my folks. Still, with Papa Karnofsky's help, I had scraped together about 10 dollars.

I looked high and low for a horn, but even the saddest ones were priced too high.

This was my last stop. I had money in my pocket to spend if the price was right.

Maybe, just maybe, my luck would change.

How much is this horn, mister?

But it's all dented.

Fifteen dollars.

Plays just as good with the dents as without.

He was right. The little horn was nothing to look at, but sounded just fine.

Thanks for letting me see it, sir. But I've only got 10 dollars.

Ten bucks, eh?

The pawnshop owner must have seen how much I wanted that horn.

The first night I worked, I made fifteen cents. I spent my nights making music, but I didn't give up my coal wagon job either.

And I was still learning the musician's trade.

When I wasn't playing, I was listening to other musicians.

You sounded great tonight, Joe.

Thanks, kid.

Joe Oliver has always been my inspiration and my idol ... when Joe would get through playing, I'd carry his horn.

Joe gave me cornet lessons.

No, Satchelmouth, try holding your lips like this.

Everyone called me Satchelmouth, which later was shortened to "Satchmo." Some people think they were making fun of me, but I disagree.

My so-called "big mouth" allowed me to play longer and better. It helped with my singing too.

Years passed, and I kept improving. I even became a member of the Tuxedo Brass Band. Everybody wanted to hear me play.

I had many regular gigs, including with orchestras for steamboats on the Mississippi River.

My opening night at the Lincoln Gardens dance hall was magic. I felt like I was at home.

We cracked down on the first note and that band sounded so good to me ... the first number went down so well we had to take an encore.

After the floor show was over and they went into some dance tunes the crowd yelled:

Let the youngster blow!

I had hit the big time. I was up North with the greats. I was playing with my idol, the King, Joe Oliver.

My boyhood dream had come true at last.

Playing in Chicago was just the beginning. Our band went on tour and I got to see America.

I made some of my first records with Joe Oliver. All of us were thrilled to be recorded at last.

But staying put in someone else's studio meant, I'd never be in control of my music.

In 1924 Joe and I parted as friends. I moved to New York City. I played and recorded with many bands and blues singers.

Still, I missed Chicago. So, I came back, and began recording as the leader of "Louis Armstrong and His Hot Five."

In 1926 we recorded "Heebie Jeebies." I did some scat singing, which proved to be popular.

I got the heebies
I got the heebie jeebies
And I'm talking about
Got the Heebie Jeebie Blues ...

But I wasn't cut out to be a band leader. I wanted to play music, not be the boss.

... and that was Louis Armstrong and his Hot Five with the jazz number, "West End Blues."

I stayed in Chicago and did lots of radio shows.

I even made it to Broadway in an all-black musical review called *Hot Chocolates.*

I ended up recording one of the songs from the show. "Ain't Misbehavin'" by Fats Waller became my best-selling record.

No one to talk with, all by myself, No one to walk with, but I'm happy on the shelf! Ain't misbehavin' ...

I also spent time in California making movies, such as *Pennies From Heaven* with Bing Crosby.

... When the skeleton in the closet started to dance!

In 1948 I appeared on Ed Sullivan's *Talk of the Town* television show for the first time.

Ladies and Gentleman, Mr. Louis Armstrong!

All through the 1930s and 1940s, I watched jazz grow in popularity. People of all kinds were interested in hearing the music.

In 1949 I became the first jazz musician ever to appear on the cover of *Time* magazine.

Old Satchmo on the cover of *Time*. I still can't believe it!

Seems the country was becoming more accepting of who you were.

The color of your skin didn't seem as important.

Still, a lot of people felt differently. One night in 1957, I was playing a concert in Knoxville, Tennessee.

The group was wailing on "Back O' Town Blues" when the entire theater shook.

WHA-BOOM!

Some fools from the White Citizens Council tossed a stick of dynamite at the theater.

Guess they didn't like having a black and white audience watching my show together, even if they were segregated. Luckily, no one was hurt.

That's all right, folks, it's just the phone.

I always kept race out of my music. But I believed in the civil rights movement.

chmo' Tells Off Ike,

Later that same year, during the attempt to desegregate in Little Rock, Arkansas, I finally said my piece.

My people ... are not looking for anything. We just want a square shake.

But when I see on television and read about a crowd in Arkansas spitting on a little colored girl, I think I have the right to get sore.

I think President Eisenhower listened.

The president has sent 1,200 National Guardsmen to escort the nine colored students to Central High School here in Little Rock.

In 1960 I toured Africa as part of a four-month trip sponsored by the U.S. State Department.

I was carried into the stadium in the Congo like a visiting king. I even stopped a civil war for a day. Both sides in the Congo Crisis called a temporary truce to hear me perform.

Towards the end of 1963, my manager gave me a song to record from a new Broadway musical.

To be honest, I didn't think much of the tune. I sang it, played a horn solo, and then forgot all about it.

WELL, HELLO, DOLLY! IT'S SO NICE TO HAVE YOU BACK WHERE YOU BELONG ...

On May 9th, 1964, "Hello, Dolly!" went to number one on the charts.

I knocked The Beatles down to number two.

A few years later, and I was singing the song to Miss Barbra Streisand in the movie *Hello, Dolly!*

I was busier than ever, and that was OK with this cat.

People are quick to forget you if you don't keep your name before the public.

Beth Israel Hospital,
New York City, March 1969

I think I've had a beautiful life so far.

Louis?
Are you sleeping?

I never wished for anything I couldn't get, and I got pretty near everything I wanted because I worked for it.

I don't care about anyone's personal lives. I'm just interested in the music.

Just want to say that music has no age. Most of your great composers—musicians—are elderly people, way up there in age—they will live forever.

As long as you are still doing something interesting and good, you are in business as long as you are breathing.

There's no such thing as on the way out.

I SEE TREES OF GREEN,
RED ROSES TOO
I SEE THEM BLOOM FOR ME
AND YOU
AND I THINK TO MYSELF ...
WHAT A WONDERFUL WORLD.

Louis Armstrong continued to give performances around the world. In March 1971, he played a final two week series of shows at the Waldorf-Astoria in New York City. On July 6, 1971, the great Satchmo died peacefully in his sleep.

Satchmo's Legacy

Louis
ARMSTRONG
PLAYS Selmer
TRUMPET Exclusively

LOUIS ARMSTRONG

LOUIS ARMSTRONG was born in New Orleans, Louisiana, on August 4, 1901. He was the only son of Willie and Mary Ann Armstrong. His father abandoned the family soon after Louis was born. Louis' early life was one of extreme poverty. His family lived in the worst part of New Orleans, in a neighborhood called The Battlefield.

Louis was forced to grow up quickly. He quit school in the third grade. He took any and all odd jobs to help support his family. An energetic boy with a wide smile, Louis later recalled enjoying his childhood despite the circumstances. He also remembered hearing jazz music playing from nearby clubs and dance halls.

As time passed, he formed a quartet that sang on corners for pennies. Louis knew that one day he would make a living from music. However, his first real training came in 1913, when he was sent to the Waifs' Home.

After his release from the home, Louis began his professional music career. His trademark gravelly voice and playful delivery was as unmistakable as his trumpet playing. By using his quick sense of humor and boyish smile, Louis grew in popularity with audiences both black and white.

He made film, radio, and TV appearances on a regular basis. He began touring the world, often serving as an unofficial "good will ambassador" for the United States. In the decades to come, he would be known to a younger generation more for his singing abilities than as an instrumentalist.

With this later success in life came increasing hospital stays and ailing periods of recovery at home. Despite health setbacks, Louis continued to tour and perform up until his death on July 6, 1971.

GLOSSARY

blues (BLOOZ)—a style of slow, sad music created by African-Americans

civil rights (SI-vil RYTS)—the rights that all people have to freedom and equal treatment under the law

encore (AHN-kor)—a song played after a band ends the main part of a concert

gig (GIG)—a live performance in front of an audience

jazz (JAZ)—a lively, rhythmical type of music in which players often make up their own tunes and add new notes in unexpected places

orchestra (OR-kuh-struh)—a large group of musicians who play their instruments together

pawnshop (PAWN-shop)—a shop where people can leave a valuable item in return for a loan; the item is returned if the loan is paid back, otherwise items are sold to other customers

scat (SKAT)—a type of singing in which the singer imitates a jazz instrument vocally without words

segregate (SEG-ruh-gate)—to keep people of different races apart in schools and other public places

READ MORE

Fahlenkamp-Merrell, Kindle. *Louis Armstrong.* Journey to Freedom. Mankato, Minn.: Child's World, 2010.

Tougas, Shelley. *Little Rock Girl 1957: How a Photograph Changed the Fight for Integration.* Captured History. Mankato, Minn.: Compass Point Books, 2012.

INTERNET SITES

FactHound offers a safe, fun way to find Internet sites related to this book. All of the sites on FactHound have been researched by our staff.

Here's all you do:

Visit www.facthound.com

Type in this code: 9781429686228

Super-cool stuff!

Check out projects, games and lots more at
www.capstonekids.com

AMERICAN GRAPHIC

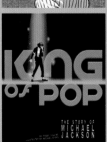